2

My Daddy

3

Draw or stick a picture of your daddy here.

LADYBIRD BOOKS

UK | USA | Canada | Ireland | Australia | India | New Zealand | South Africa

Ladybird Books is part of the Penguin Random House group of companies
whose addresses can be found at global.penguinrandomhouse.com.

www.penguin.co.uk   www.puffin.co.uk   www.ladybird.co.uk

Penguin
Random House
UK

First published 2019
001

This book copyright © Astley Baker Davies Ltd/Entertainment One UK Ltd 2019
Adapted by Lauren Holowaty

This book is based on the TV series *Peppa Pig*.
Peppa Pig is created by Neville Astley and Mark Baker.
Peppa Pig © Astley Baker Davies Ltd/Entertainment One UK Ltd 2003.
www.peppapig.com

Printed in China

A CIP catalogue record for this book is available from the British Library

ISBN: 978-0-241-37157-2

All correspondence to:
Ladybird Books
Penguin Random House Children's
80 Strand, London WC2R 0RL

"What are we doing today, Daddy?"
asked Peppa one morning.
"Today," said Daddy Pig, "we're going
on a **surprise** adventure!"

"Ooooh!" gasped Peppa and George,
bouncing up and down in their seats.

When Daddy Pig had everything ready, he called Peppa and George. "Are you ready for your *dad*-venture?" he asked.
"Yes, Daddy!" they cried, giggling.

Hee! Hee! Hee!

"First stop – the *supermarket*!" said Daddy Pig.
"That doesn't sound very adventury," said Peppa.
"You'll see," Daddy Pig replied.

Daddy Pig zoomed around the supermarket with the trolley. "This is how you shop . . . in style!" he cried, dancing and juggling with the food, then rolling the tins down his arm and into the trolley.

Peppa and George clapped their hands. "Go, Daddy!"

Beep!

Peppa, George and Daddy Pig filled the trolley to the very top. Plunk! Plop! Crash! "I think that's everything," said Daddy Pig. "I think that's everything in the shop!" said Miss Rabbit.

"Daddy," said Peppa as they
put the food in the car, "I love
shopping . . . in style!"
"Me too," agreed Daddy Pig.

"Next stop – lunch with Granny and
Grandpa Pig," announced Daddy Pig.
"Lunch isn't an adventure, Daddy,"
said Peppa. "We have lunch every day."

"Yes, but do you have it on a *pirate ship*?" asked Daddy Pig.
"No," said Peppa.
"*Arrrr!*" cried George in his best pirate voice.

Everybody hopped on board the ship for
a special pirate picnic made by Daddy Pig.
"Goodness," said Grandpa Pig. "This delicious
food is worthy of the captain's table!"

"Daddy," said Peppa, "I love pirate picnics!"
"Me too," said Daddy Pig, munching away.

"Where are you off to next, my little pirates?" asked Granny Pig.
"I need to do a spot of work," said Daddy Pig.
"Oh!" sighed Peppa. "Work's boring, Daddy."

"Not *my* work, Peppa," said Daddy Pig. "My work is an adventure!" He pointed over to Miss Rabbit, who was waiting for them in her helicopter . . .

"Ready to fly to work, Daddy Pig?" asked Miss Rabbit.
"We are indeed," said Daddy Pig.
"Wow!" gasped Peppa and George, buckling up.
They waved goodbye to Granny and Grandpa Pig,
and then Miss Rabbit zoomed them across the sky.

"Daddy!" called Peppa over the noise of the helicopter. "I love going to work!"
"Me too!" called Daddy Pig.

Miss Rabbit landed the helicopter at the playground.
"First, all the holes need filling with concrete," said Daddy Pig.
Peppa and George sat in the driver's seat of a big, loud truck
and poured concrete all over the playground!

"Daddy!" shouted Peppa. "I love pouring concrete!"
"Me too!" Daddy Pig shouted back.

"And now it's time to test all the play equipment to make sure it works," said Daddy Pig.

"Hooray!" cheered Peppa, running to the seesaw.

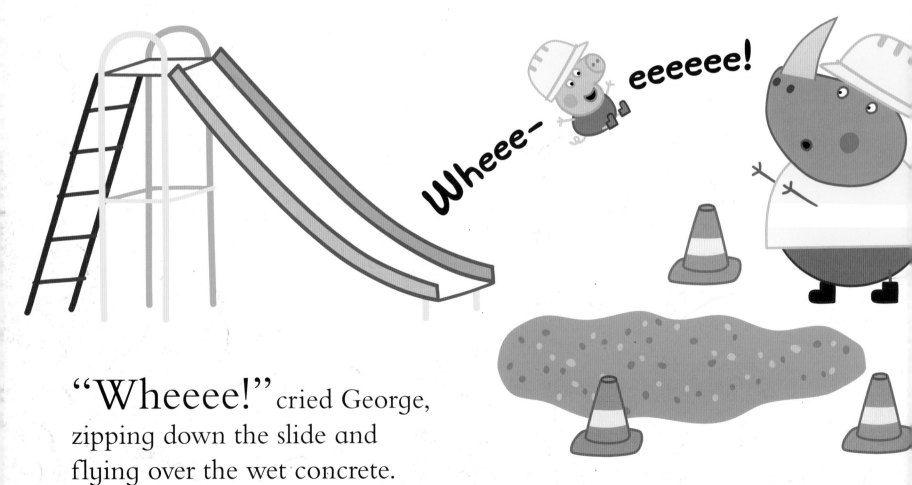

Wheee-eeeeee!

"Wheeee!" cried George, zipping down the slide and flying over the wet concrete.

"Where to next, Daddy Pig?" asked Miss Rabbit.
"The fair, please," said Daddy Pig.
"Rightio," said Miss Rabbit.

At the fair, Peppa, George and Daddy Pig filled all the holes with concrete. Then they tested all the rides . . . twice!

"Daddy," said Peppa,
"I **love** the fair!"

"Me too!" agreed
Daddy Pig.

"We have one last job," said Daddy Pig.
"We must sign our work."
Peppa, George and Daddy Pig gently
pressed their hands into the wet concrete.

"Now everyone will know who poured
this amazing concrete!" said Peppa.

Miss Rabbit flew everyone back to the car.
"Daddy!" shouted Peppa. "I love your job!"
"Me too!" agreed Daddy Pig.

When they got home, Mummy Pig asked Daddy Pig how their day was.

"Oh, just a normal day, really," said Daddy Pig. "We did a little shopping, had some lunch with Granny and Grandpa Pig, and then I had to do a spot of work." He winked at Peppa and George.
Peppa and George winked back at him.

After their baths, Daddy Pig tucked Peppa and George into bed.
"Daddy," said Peppa, "I love . . ." Peppa stopped to yawn.
"Yes, Peppa?" said Daddy Pig.
"I love . . . you, Daddy!" said Peppa.
"I love you, too," said Daddy Pig. "I love *both* my little adventurers!"

After such a busy day, the two little adventurers soon fell fast asleep.

"Daddy Pig," said Mummy Pig
when he came back downstairs,
"what are these?"
She held up the pirate costumes,
hard hats and photos from the
rides at the fair.

"I thought you spent the day shopping, having lunch
with Granny and Grandpa Pig, and doing some work?"

"Well . . ." said Daddy Pig, and then he told Mummy Pig all about his day.

Mummy Pig was very impressed. "I love you, Daddy Pig," she said.

"You make every day an adventure!"